The Re-Gifter's Tracking Book

Kay D Johnson

Copyright © 2018 by Kay D. Johnson

Johnson, Kay D
The Re-Gifter's Tracking Book

ISBN 978-1-989194-90-4 (pbk)

The Re-Gifter's Tracking Book

Gift Received:

Event Received:

Received From:

Date:

Re-Gifted To:

Event Re-Gifted:

Date:

Got the Same Gift Back: No ... Great!

: Yes ... See Page #   to start over.

Gift Received:

Event Received:

Received From:

Date:

Re-Gifted To:

Event Re-Gifted:

Date:

Got the Same Gift Back: No ... Great!

: Yes ... See Page #   to start over.

Gift Received:

Event Received:

Received From:

Date:

Re-Gifted To:

Event Re-Gifted:

Date:

Got the Same Gift Back: No ... Great!

: Yes ... See Page #   to start over.

The Re-Gifter's Tracking Book

Gift Received:

Event Received:

Received From:

Date:

Re-Gifted To:

Event Re-Gifted:

Date:

Got the Same Gift Back: No ... Great!

: Yes ... See Page #   to start over.

Gift Received:

Event Received:

Received From:

Date:

Re-Gifted To:

Event Re-Gifted:

Date:

Got the Same Gift Back: No ... Great!

: Yes ... See Page #   to start over.

Gift Received:

Event Received:

Received From:

Date:

Re-Gifted To:

Event Re-Gifted:

Date:

Got the Same Gift Back: No ... Great!

: Yes ... See Page #   to start over.

The Re-Gifter's Tracking Book

Gift Received:
_____

Event Received:
_____

Received From:
_____

Date:
_____

Re-Gifted To:
_____

Event Re-Gifted:
_____

Date:
_____

Got the Same Gift Back: No ... Great!
_____
     : Yes ... See Page #   to start over.

Gift Received:
_____

Event Received:
_____

Received From:
_____

Date:
_____

Re-Gifted To:
_____

Event Re-Gifted:
_____

Date:
_____

Got the Same Gift Back: No ... Great!
_____
     : Yes ... See Page #   to start over.

Gift Received:
_____

Event Received:
_____

Received From:
_____

Date:
_____

Re-Gifted To:
_____

Event Re-Gifted:
_____

Date:
_____

Got the Same Gift Back: No ... Great!
_____
     : Yes ... See Page #   to start over.

The Re-Gifter's Tracking Book

Gift Received:
_____

Event Received:
_____

Received From:
_____

Date:
_____

Re-Gifted To:
_____

Event Re-Gifted:
_____

Date:
_____

Got the Same Gift Back: No ... Great!

_____ : Yes ... See Page #_____ to start over.

Gift Received:
_____

Event Received:
_____

Received From:
_____

Date:
_____

Re-Gifted To:
_____

Event Re-Gifted:
_____

Date:
_____

Got the Same Gift Back: No ... Great!

_____ : Yes ... See Page #_____ to start over.

Gift Received:
_____

Event Received:
_____

Received From:
_____

Date:
_____

Re-Gifted To:
_____

Event Re-Gifted:
_____

Date:
_____

Got the Same Gift Back: No ... Great!

_____ : Yes ... See Page #_____ to start over.

The Re-Gifter's Tracking Book

Gift Received:
_____

Event Received:
_____

Received From:
_____

Date:
_____

Re-Gifted To:
_____

Event Re-Gifted:
_____

Date:
_____

Got the Same Gift Back: No ... Great!
_____
: Yes ... See Page # _____ to start over.

Gift Received:
_____

Event Received:
_____

Received From:
_____

Date:
_____

Re-Gifted To:
_____

Event Re-Gifted:
_____

Date:
_____

Got the Same Gift Back: No ... Great!
_____
: Yes ... See Page # _____ to start over.

Gift Received:
_____

Event Received:
_____

Received From:
_____

Date:
_____

Re-Gifted To:
_____

Event Re-Gifted:
_____

Date:
_____

Got the Same Gift Back: No ... Great!
_____
: Yes ... See Page # _____ to start over.

The Re-Gifter's Tracking Book

Gift Received:
_____
Event Received:
_____
Received From:
_____
Date:
_____
Re-Gifted To:
_____
Event Re-Gifted:
_____
Date:
_____
Got the Same Gift Back: No ... Great!
_____
      : Yes ... See Page # to start over.
_____

Gift Received:
_____
Event Received:
_____
Received From:
_____
Date:
_____
Re-Gifted To:
_____
Event Re-Gifted:
_____
Date:
_____
Got the Same Gift Back: No ... Great!
_____
      : Yes ... See Page # to start over.
_____

Gift Received:
_____
Event Received:
_____
Received From:
_____
Date:
_____
Re-Gifted To:
_____
Event Re-Gifted:
_____
Date:
_____
Got the Same Gift Back: No ... Great!
_____
      : Yes ... See Page # to start over.
_____

The Re-Gifter's Tracking Book

Gift Received:
_____

Event Received:
_____

Received From:
_____

Date:
_____

Re-Gifted To:
_____

Event Re-Gifted:
_____

Date:
_____

Got the Same Gift Back: No ... Great!
_____

                : Yes ... See Page #   to start over.

Gift Received:
_____

Event Received:
_____

Received From:
_____

Date:
_____

Re-Gifted To:
_____

Event Re-Gifted:
_____

Date:
_____

Got the Same Gift Back: No ... Great!
_____

                : Yes ... See Page #   to start over.

Gift Received:
_____

Event Received:
_____

Received From:
_____

Date:
_____

Re-Gifted To:
_____

Event Re-Gifted:
_____

Date:
_____

Got the Same Gift Back: No ... Great!
_____

                : Yes ... See Page #   to start over.

The Re-Gifter's Tracking Book

Gift Received:

Event Received:

Received From:

Date:

Re-Gifted To:

Event Re-Gifted:

Date:

Got the Same Gift Back: No ... Great!

: Yes ... See Page #   to start over.

Gift Received:

Event Received:

Received From:

Date:

Re-Gifted To:

Event Re-Gifted:

Date:

Got the Same Gift Back: No ... Great!

: Yes ... See Page #   to start over.

Gift Received:

Event Received:

Received From:

Date:

Re-Gifted To:

Event Re-Gifted:

Date:

Got the Same Gift Back: No ... Great!

: Yes ... See Page #   to start over.

The Re-Gifter's Tracking Book

Gift Received:
_____

Event Received:
_____

Received From:
_____

Date:
_____

Re-Gifted To:
_____

Event Re-Gifted:
_____

Date:
_____

Got the Same Gift Back: No ... Great!

: Yes ... See Page #_____ to start over.

Gift Received:
_____

Event Received:
_____

Received From:
_____

Date:
_____

Re-Gifted To:
_____

Event Re-Gifted:
_____

Date:
_____

Got the Same Gift Back: No ... Great!

: Yes ... See Page #_____ to start over.

Gift Received:
_____

Event Received:
_____

Received From:
_____

Date:
_____

Re-Gifted To:
_____

Event Re-Gifted:
_____

Date:
_____

Got the Same Gift Back: No ... Great!

: Yes ... See Page #_____ to start over.

The Re-Gifter's Tracking Book

Gift Received:
_____

Event Received:
_____

Received From:
_____

Date:
_____

Re-Gifted To:
_____

Event Re-Gifted:
_____

Date:
_____

Got the Same Gift Back: No ... Great!
_____

               : Yes ... See Page #_____ to start over.
_____

Gift Received:
_____

Event Received:
_____

Received From:
_____

Date:
_____

Re-Gifted To:
_____

Event Re-Gifted:
_____

Date:
_____

Got the Same Gift Back: No ... Great!
_____

               : Yes ... See Page #_____ to start over.
_____

Gift Received:
_____

Event Received:
_____

Received From:
_____

Date:
_____

Re-Gifted To:
_____

Event Re-Gifted:
_____

Date:
_____

Got the Same Gift Back: No ... Great!
_____

               : Yes ... See Page #_____ to start over.
_____

The Re-Gifter's Tracking Book

Gift Received:
_____

Event Received:
_____

Received From:
_____

Date:
_____

Re-Gifted To:
_____

Event Re-Gifted:
_____

Date:
_____

Got the Same Gift Back: No ... Great!
_____

                  : Yes ... See Page # _____ to start over.

Gift Received:
_____

Event Received:
_____

Received From:
_____

Date:
_____

Re-Gifted To:
_____

Event Re-Gifted:
_____

Date:
_____

Got the Same Gift Back: No ... Great!
_____

                  : Yes ... See Page # _____ to start over.

Gift Received:
_____

Event Received:
_____

Received From:
_____

Date:
_____

Re-Gifted To:
_____

Event Re-Gifted:
_____

Date:
_____

Got the Same Gift Back: No ... Great!
_____

                  : Yes ... See Page # _____ to start over.

The Re-Gifter's Tracking Book

Gift Received:
_____

Event Received:
_____

Received From:
_____

Date:
_____

Re-Gifted To:
_____

Event Re-Gifted:
_____

Date:
_____

Got the Same Gift Back: No ... Great!

                 : Yes ... See Page #   to start over.

Gift Received:
_____

Event Received:
_____

Received From:
_____

Date:
_____

Re-Gifted To:
_____

Event Re-Gifted:
_____

Date:
_____

Got the Same Gift Back: No ... Great!

                 : Yes ... See Page #   to start over.

Gift Received:
_____

Event Received:
_____

Received From:
_____

Date:
_____

Re-Gifted To:
_____

Event Re-Gifted:
_____

Date:
_____

Got the Same Gift Back: No ... Great!

                 : Yes ... See Page #   to start over.

The Re-Gifter's Tracking Book

Gift Received:
_____

Event Received:
_____

Received From:
_____

Date:
_____

Re-Gifted To:
_____

Event Re-Gifted:
_____

Date:
_____

Got the Same Gift Back: No ... Great!
_____

: Yes ... See Page #_____ to start over.

Gift Received:
_____

Event Received:
_____

Received From:
_____

Date:
_____

Re-Gifted To:
_____

Event Re-Gifted:
_____

Date:
_____

Got the Same Gift Back: No ... Great!
_____

: Yes ... See Page #_____ to start over.

Gift Received:
_____

Event Received:
_____

Received From:
_____

Date:
_____

Re-Gifted To:
_____

Event Re-Gifted:
_____

Date:
_____

Got the Same Gift Back: No ... Great!
_____

: Yes ... See Page #_____ to start over.

The Re-Gifter's Tracking Book

Gift Received:
_____

Event Received:
_____

Received From:
_____

Date:
_____

Re-Gifted To:
_____

Event Re-Gifted:
_____

Date:
_____

Got the Same Gift Back: No ... Great!

: Yes ... See Page #_____ to start over.

Gift Received:
_____

Event Received:
_____

Received From:
_____

Date:
_____

Re-Gifted To:
_____

Event Re-Gifted:
_____

Date:
_____

Got the Same Gift Back: No ... Great!

: Yes ... See Page #_____ to start over.

Gift Received:
_____

Event Received:
_____

Received From:
_____

Date:
_____

Re-Gifted To:
_____

Event Re-Gifted:
_____

Date:
_____

Got the Same Gift Back: No ... Great!

: Yes ... See Page #_____ to start over.

The Re-Gifter's Tracking Book

Gift Received:

Event Received:

Received From:

Date:

Re-Gifted To:

Event Re-Gifted:

Date:

Got the Same Gift Back: No ... Great!

: Yes ... See Page #   to start over.

Gift Received:

Event Received:

Received From:

Date:

Re-Gifted To:

Event Re-Gifted:

Date:

Got the Same Gift Back: No ... Great!

: Yes ... See Page #   to start over.

Gift Received:

Event Received:

Received From:

Date:

Re-Gifted To:

Event Re-Gifted:

Date:

Got the Same Gift Back: No ... Great!

: Yes ... See Page #   to start over.

The Re-Gifter's Tracking Book

Gift Received:

Event Received:

Received From:

Date:

Re-Gifted To:

Event Re-Gifted:

Date:

Got the Same Gift Back: No ... Great!

: Yes ... See Page #   to start over.

Gift Received:

Event Received:

Received From:

Date:

Re-Gifted To:

Event Re-Gifted:

Date:

Got the Same Gift Back: No ... Great!

: Yes ... See Page #   to start over.

Gift Received:

Event Received:

Received From:

Date:

Re-Gifted To:

Event Re-Gifted:

Date:

Got the Same Gift Back: No ... Great!

: Yes ... See Page #   to start over.

The Re-Gifter's Tracking Book

Gift Received:

Event Received:

Received From:

Date:

Re-Gifted To:

Event Re-Gifted:

Date:

Got the Same Gift Back: No ... Great!

: Yes ... See Page #   to start over.

Gift Received:

Event Received:

Received From:

Date:

Re-Gifted To:

Event Re-Gifted:

Date:

Got the Same Gift Back: No ... Great!

: Yes ... See Page #   to start over.

Gift Received:

Event Received:

Received From:

Date:

Re-Gifted To:

Event Re-Gifted:

Date:

Got the Same Gift Back: No ... Great!

: Yes ... See Page #   to start over.

The Re-Gifter's Tracking Book

Gift Received:
_____
Event Received:
_____
Received From:
_____
Date:
_____
Re-Gifted To:
_____
Event Re-Gifted:
_____
Date:
_____
Got the Same Gift Back: No ... Great!

                : Yes ... See Page #   to start over.
_____

Gift Received:
_____
Event Received:
_____
Received From:
_____
Date:
_____
Re-Gifted To:
_____
Event Re-Gifted:
_____
Date:
_____
Got the Same Gift Back: No ... Great!

                : Yes ... See Page #   to start over.
_____

Gift Received:
_____
Event Received:
_____
Received From:
_____
Date:
_____
Re-Gifted To:
_____
Event Re-Gifted:
_____
Date:
_____
Got the Same Gift Back: No ... Great!

                : Yes ... See Page #   to start over.

The Re-Gifter's Tracking Book

Gift Received:
_____

Event Received:
_____

Received From:
_____

Date:
_____

Re-Gifted To:
_____

Event Re-Gifted:
_____

Date:
_____

Got the Same Gift Back: No ... Great!

          : Yes ... See Page #   to start over.

Gift Received:
_____

Event Received:
_____

Received From:
_____

Date:
_____

Re-Gifted To:
_____

Event Re-Gifted:
_____

Date:
_____

Got the Same Gift Back: No ... Great!

          : Yes ... See Page #   to start over.

Gift Received:
_____

Event Received:
_____

Received From:
_____

Date:
_____

Re-Gifted To:
_____

Event Re-Gifted:
_____

Date:
_____

Got the Same Gift Back: No ... Great!

          : Yes ... See Page #   to start over.

The Re-Gifter's Tracking Book

Gift Received:
_____

Event Received:
_____

Received From:
_____

Date:
_____

Re-Gifted To:
_____

Event Re-Gifted:
_____

Date:
_____

Got the Same Gift Back: No ... Great!

: Yes ... See Page #   to start over.
_____

Gift Received:
_____

Event Received:
_____

Received From:
_____

Date:
_____

Re-Gifted To:
_____

Event Re-Gifted:
_____

Date:
_____

Got the Same Gift Back: No ... Great!

: Yes ... See Page #   to start over.
_____

Gift Received:
_____

Event Received:
_____

Received From:
_____

Date:
_____

Re-Gifted To:
_____

Event Re-Gifted:
_____

Date:
_____

Got the Same Gift Back: No ... Great!

: Yes ... See Page #   to start over.
_____

The Re-Gifter's Tracking Book

Gift Received:
_____

Event Received:
_____

Received From:
_____

Date:
_____

Re-Gifted To:
_____

Event Re-Gifted:
_____

Date:
_____

Got the Same Gift Back: No ... Great!

: Yes ... See Page #   to start over.

Gift Received:
_____

Event Received:
_____

Received From:
_____

Date:
_____

Re-Gifted To:
_____

Event Re-Gifted:
_____

Date:
_____

Got the Same Gift Back: No ... Great!

: Yes ... See Page #   to start over.

Gift Received:
_____

Event Received:
_____

Received From:
_____

Date:
_____

Re-Gifted To:
_____

Event Re-Gifted:
_____

Date:
_____

Got the Same Gift Back: No ... Great!

: Yes ... See Page #   to start over.

The Re-Gifter's Tracking Book

Gift Received:

Event Received:

Received From:

Date:

Re-Gifted To:

Event Re-Gifted:

Date:

Got the Same Gift Back: No ... Great!

: Yes ... See Page #   to start over.

Gift Received:

Event Received:

Received From:

Date:

Re-Gifted To:

Event Re-Gifted:

Date:

Got the Same Gift Back: No ... Great!

: Yes ... See Page #   to start over.

Gift Received:

Event Received:

Received From:

Date:

Re-Gifted To:

Event Re-Gifted:

Date:

Got the Same Gift Back: No ... Great!

: Yes ... See Page #   to start over.

The Re-Gifter's Tracking Book

Gift Received:
_____

Event Received:
_____

Received From:
_____

Date:
_____

Re-Gifted To:
_____

Event Re-Gifted:
_____

Date:
_____

Got the Same Gift Back: No ... Great!

: Yes ... See Page #_____ to start over.

Gift Received:
_____

Event Received:
_____

Received From:
_____

Date:
_____

Re-Gifted To:
_____

Event Re-Gifted:
_____

Date:
_____

Got the Same Gift Back: No ... Great!

: Yes ... See Page #_____ to start over.

Gift Received:
_____

Event Received:
_____

Received From:
_____

Date:
_____

Re-Gifted To:
_____

Event Re-Gifted:
_____

Date:
_____

Got the Same Gift Back: No ... Great!

: Yes ... See Page #_____ to start over.

The Re-Gifter's Tracking Book

Gift Received:
_____

Event Received:
_____

Received From:
_____

Date:
_____

Re-Gifted To:
_____

Event Re-Gifted:
_____

Date:
_____

Got the Same Gift Back: No ... Great!

                 : Yes ... See Page #   to start over.
_____

Gift Received:
_____

Event Received:
_____

Received From:
_____

Date:
_____

Re-Gifted To:
_____

Event Re-Gifted:
_____

Date:
_____

Got the Same Gift Back: No ... Great!

                 : Yes ... See Page #   to start over.
_____

Gift Received:
_____

Event Received:
_____

Received From:
_____

Date:
_____

Re-Gifted To:
_____

Event Re-Gifted:
_____

Date:
_____

Got the Same Gift Back: No ... Great!

                 : Yes ... See Page #   to start over.

The Re-Gifter's Tracking Book

Gift Received:

Event Received:

Received From:

Date:

Re-Gifted To:

Event Re-Gifted:

Date:

Got the Same Gift Back: No ... Great!

                  : Yes ... See Page #   to start over.

Gift Received:

Event Received:

Received From:

Date:

Re-Gifted To:

Event Re-Gifted:

Date:

Got the Same Gift Back: No ... Great!

                  : Yes ... See Page #   to start over.

Gift Received:

Event Received:

Received From:

Date:

Re-Gifted To:

Event Re-Gifted:

Date:

Got the Same Gift Back: No ... Great!

                  : Yes ... See Page #   to start over.

The Re-Gifter's Tracking Book

Gift Received:
_____
Event Received:
_____
Received From:
_____
Date:
_____
Re-Gifted To:
_____
Event Re-Gifted:
_____
Date:
_____
Got the Same Gift Back: No ... Great!
_____
: Yes ... See Page # _____ to start over.

Gift Received:
_____
Event Received:
_____
Received From:
_____
Date:
_____
Re-Gifted To:
_____
Event Re-Gifted:
_____
Date:
_____
Got the Same Gift Back: No ... Great!
_____
: Yes ... See Page # _____ to start over.

Gift Received:
_____
Event Received:
_____
Received From:
_____
Date:
_____
Re-Gifted To:
_____
Event Re-Gifted:
_____
Date:
_____
Got the Same Gift Back: No ... Great!
_____
: Yes ... See Page # _____ to start over.

The Re-Gifter's Tracking Book

Gift Received:

Event Received:

Received From:

Date:

Re-Gifted To:

Event Re-Gifted:

Date:

Got the Same Gift Back: No ... Great!

                        : Yes ... See Page #   to start over.

Gift Received:

Event Received:

Received From:

Date:

Re-Gifted To:

Event Re-Gifted:

Date:

Got the Same Gift Back: No ... Great!

                        : Yes ... See Page #   to start over.

Gift Received:

Event Received:

Received From:

Date:

Re-Gifted To:

Event Re-Gifted:

Date:

Got the Same Gift Back: No ... Great!

                        : Yes ... See Page #   to start over.

The Re-Gifter's Tracking Book

Gift Received:
_____

Event Received:
_____

Received From:
_____

Date:
_____

Re-Gifted To:
_____

Event Re-Gifted:
_____

Date:
_____

Got the Same Gift Back: No ... Great!

: Yes ... See Page #_____ to start over.

Gift Received:
_____

Event Received:
_____

Received From:
_____

Date:
_____

Re-Gifted To:
_____

Event Re-Gifted:
_____

Date:
_____

Got the Same Gift Back: No ... Great!

: Yes ... See Page #_____ to start over.

Gift Received:
_____

Event Received:
_____

Received From:
_____

Date:
_____

Re-Gifted To:
_____

Event Re-Gifted:
_____

Date:
_____

Got the Same Gift Back: No ... Great!

: Yes ... See Page #_____ to start over.

The Re-Gifter's Tracking Book

Gift Received:

Event Received:

Received From:

Date:

Re-Gifted To:

Event Re-Gifted:

Date:

Got the Same Gift Back: No ... Great!

: Yes ... See Page #   to start over.

Gift Received:

Event Received:

Received From:

Date:

Re-Gifted To:

Event Re-Gifted:

Date:

Got the Same Gift Back: No ... Great!

: Yes ... See Page #   to start over.

Gift Received:

Event Received:

Received From:

Date:

Re-Gifted To:

Event Re-Gifted:

Date:

Got the Same Gift Back: No ... Great!

: Yes ... See Page #   to start over.

The Re-Gifter's Tracking Book

Gift Received:

Event Received:

Received From:

Date:

Re-Gifted To:

Event Re-Gifted:

Date:

Got the Same Gift Back: No ... Great!

: Yes ... See Page #   to start over.

Gift Received:

Event Received:

Received From:

Date:

Re-Gifted To:

Event Re-Gifted:

Date:

Got the Same Gift Back: No ... Great!

: Yes ... See Page #   to start over.

Gift Received:

Event Received:

Received From:

Date:

Re-Gifted To:

Event Re-Gifted:

Date:

Got the Same Gift Back: No ... Great!

: Yes ... See Page #   to start over.

The Re-Gifter's Tracking Book

Gift Received: _____

Event Received: _____

Received From: _____

Date: _____

Re-Gifted To: _____

Event Re-Gifted: _____

Date: _____

Got the Same Gift Back: No ... Great!

                        : Yes ... See Page #_____ to start over.

Gift Received: _____

Event Received: _____

Received From: _____

Date: _____

Re-Gifted To: _____

Event Re-Gifted: _____

Date: _____

Got the Same Gift Back: No ... Great!

                        : Yes ... See Page #_____ to start over.

Gift Received: _____

Event Received: _____

Received From: _____

Date: _____

Re-Gifted To: _____

Event Re-Gifted: _____

Date: _____

Got the Same Gift Back: No ... Great!

                        : Yes ... See Page #_____ to start over.

The Re-Gifter's Tracking Book

Gift Received:

Event Received:

Received From:

Date:

Re-Gifted To:

Event Re-Gifted:

Date:

Got the Same Gift Back: No ... Great!

: Yes ... See Page #   to start over.

Gift Received:

Event Received:

Received From:

Date:

Re-Gifted To:

Event Re-Gifted:

Date:

Got the Same Gift Back: No ... Great!

: Yes ... See Page #   to start over.

Gift Received:

Event Received:

Received From:

Date:

Re-Gifted To:

Event Re-Gifted:

Date:

Got the Same Gift Back: No ... Great!

: Yes ... See Page #   to start over.

The Re-Gifter's Tracking Book

Gift Received:
_____
Event Received:
_____
Received From:
_____
Date:
_____
Re-Gifted To:
_____
Event Re-Gifted:
_____
Date:
_____
Got the Same Gift Back: No ... Great!
: Yes ... See Page # _____ to start over.
_____

Gift Received:
_____
Event Received:
_____
Received From:
_____
Date:
_____
Re-Gifted To:
_____
Event Re-Gifted:
_____
Date:
_____
Got the Same Gift Back: No ... Great!
: Yes ... See Page # _____ to start over.
_____

Gift Received:
_____
Event Received:
_____
Received From:
_____
Date:
_____
Re-Gifted To:
_____
Event Re-Gifted:
_____
Date:
_____
Got the Same Gift Back: No ... Great!
: Yes ... See Page # _____ to start over.
_____

The Re-Gifter's Tracking Book

Gift Received:
_____
Event Received:
_____
Received From:
_____
Date:
_____
Re-Gifted To:
_____
Event Re-Gifted:
_____
Date:
_____
Got the Same Gift Back: No ... Great!
_____
          : Yes ... See Page #   to start over.
_____

Gift Received:
_____
Event Received:
_____
Received From:
_____
Date:
_____
Re-Gifted To:
_____
Event Re-Gifted:
_____
Date:
_____
Got the Same Gift Back: No ... Great!
_____
          : Yes ... See Page #   to start over.
_____

Gift Received:
_____
Event Received:
_____
Received From:
_____
Date:
_____
Re-Gifted To:
_____
Event Re-Gifted:
_____
Date:
_____
Got the Same Gift Back: No ... Great!
_____
          : Yes ... See Page #   to start over.
_____

The Re-Gifter's Tracking Book

Gift Received:
_____

Event Received:
_____

Received From:
_____

Date:
_____

Re-Gifted To:
_____

Event Re-Gifted:
_____

Date:
_____

Got the Same Gift Back: No ... Great!
_____
: Yes ... See Page #   to start over.
_____

Gift Received:
_____

Event Received:
_____

Received From:
_____

Date:
_____

Re-Gifted To:
_____

Event Re-Gifted:
_____

Date:
_____

Got the Same Gift Back: No ... Great!
_____
: Yes ... See Page #   to start over.
_____

Gift Received:
_____

Event Received:
_____

Received From:
_____

Date:
_____

Re-Gifted To:
_____

Event Re-Gifted:
_____

Date:
_____

Got the Same Gift Back: No ... Great!
_____
: Yes ... See Page #   to start over.
_____

The Re-Gifter's Tracking Book

Gift Received:

Event Received:

Received From:

Date:

Re-Gifted To:

Event Re-Gifted:

Date:

Got the Same Gift Back: No ... Great!

: Yes ... See Page #   to start over.

Gift Received:

Event Received:

Received From:

Date:

Re-Gifted To:

Event Re-Gifted:

Date:

Got the Same Gift Back: No ... Great!

: Yes ... See Page #   to start over.

Gift Received:

Event Received:

Received From:

Date:

Re-Gifted To:

Event Re-Gifted:

Date:

Got the Same Gift Back: No ... Great!

: Yes ... See Page #   to start over.

The Re-Gifter's Tracking Book

Gift Received:
_____
Event Received:
_____
Received From:
_____
Date:
_____
Re-Gifted To:
_____
Event Re-Gifted:
_____
Date:
_____
Got the Same Gift Back: No ... Great!
_____
         : Yes ... See Page #   to start over.

Gift Received:
_____
Event Received:
_____
Received From:
_____
Date:
_____
Re-Gifted To:
_____
Event Re-Gifted:
_____
Date:
_____
Got the Same Gift Back: No ... Great!
_____
         : Yes ... See Page #   to start over.

Gift Received:
_____
Event Received:
_____
Received From:
_____
Date:
_____
Re-Gifted To:
_____
Event Re-Gifted:
_____
Date:
_____
Got the Same Gift Back: No ... Great!
_____
         : Yes ... See Page #   to start over.

The Re-Gifter's Tracking Book

Gift Received:

Event Received:

Received From:

Date:

Re-Gifted To:

Event Re-Gifted:

Date:

Got the Same Gift Back: No ... Great!

: Yes ... See Page #   to start over.

Gift Received:

Event Received:

Received From:

Date:

Re-Gifted To:

Event Re-Gifted:

Date:

Got the Same Gift Back: No ... Great!

: Yes ... See Page #   to start over.

Gift Received:

Event Received:

Received From:

Date:

Re-Gifted To:

Event Re-Gifted:

Date:

Got the Same Gift Back: No ... Great!

: Yes ... See Page #   to start over.

The Re-Gifter's Tracking Book

Gift Received:
_____
Event Received:
_____
Received From:
_____
Date:
_____
Re-Gifted To:
_____
Event Re-Gifted:
_____
Date:
_____
Got the Same Gift Back: No ... Great!
                    : Yes ... See Page #   to start over.

Gift Received:
_____
Event Received:
_____
Received From:
_____
Date:
_____
Re-Gifted To:
_____
Event Re-Gifted:
_____
Date:
_____
Got the Same Gift Back: No ... Great!
                    : Yes ... See Page #   to start over.

Gift Received:
_____
Event Received:
_____
Received From:
_____
Date:
_____
Re-Gifted To:
_____
Event Re-Gifted:
_____
Date:
_____
Got the Same Gift Back: No ... Great!
                    : Yes ... See Page #   to start over.

The Re-Gifter's Tracking Book

Gift Received:
_____

Event Received:
_____

Received From:
_____

Date:
_____

Re-Gifted To:
_____

Event Re-Gifted:
_____

Date:
_____

Got the Same Gift Back: No ... Great!

: Yes ... See Page #   to start over.
_____

Gift Received:
_____

Event Received:
_____

Received From:
_____

Date:
_____

Re-Gifted To:
_____

Event Re-Gifted:
_____

Date:
_____

Got the Same Gift Back: No ... Great!

: Yes ... See Page #   to start over.
_____

Gift Received:
_____

Event Received:
_____

Received From:
_____

Date:
_____

Re-Gifted To:
_____

Event Re-Gifted:
_____

Date:
_____

Got the Same Gift Back: No ... Great!

: Yes ... See Page #   to start over.
_____

The Re-Gifter's Tracking Book

Gift Received:
_____
Event Received:
_____
Received From:
_____
Date:
_____
Re-Gifted To:
_____
Event Re-Gifted:
_____
Date:
_____
Got the Same Gift Back: No ... Great!
_____
                        : Yes ... See Page # _____ to start over.
_____

Gift Received:
_____
Event Received:
_____
Received From:
_____
Date:
_____
Re-Gifted To:
_____
Event Re-Gifted:
_____
Date:
_____
Got the Same Gift Back: No ... Great!
_____
                        : Yes ... See Page # _____ to start over.
_____

Gift Received:
_____
Event Received:
_____
Received From:
_____
Date:
_____
Re-Gifted To:
_____
Event Re-Gifted:
_____
Date:
_____
Got the Same Gift Back: No ... Great!
_____
                        : Yes ... See Page # _____ to start over.
_____

The Re-Gifter's Tracking Book

Gift Received:
_____
Event Received:
_____
Received From:
_____
Date:
_____
Re-Gifted To:
_____
Event Re-Gifted:
_____
Date:
_____
Got the Same Gift Back: No ... Great!
_____
: Yes ... See Page #   to start over.
_____

Gift Received:
_____
Event Received:
_____
Received From:
_____
Date:
_____
Re-Gifted To:
_____
Event Re-Gifted:
_____
Date:
_____
Got the Same Gift Back: No ... Great!
_____
: Yes ... See Page #   to start over.
_____

Gift Received:
_____
Event Received:
_____
Received From:
_____
Date:
_____
Re-Gifted To:
_____
Event Re-Gifted:
_____
Date:
_____
Got the Same Gift Back: No ... Great!
_____
: Yes ... See Page #   to start over.
_____

The Re-Gifter's Tracking Book

Gift Received:

Event Received:

Received From:

Date:

Re-Gifted To:

Event Re-Gifted:

Date:

Got the Same Gift Back: No ... Great!

: Yes ... See Page #   to start over.

Gift Received:

Event Received:

Received From:

Date:

Re-Gifted To:

Event Re-Gifted:

Date:

Got the Same Gift Back: No ... Great!

: Yes ... See Page #   to start over.

Gift Received:

Event Received:

Received From:

Date:

Re-Gifted To:

Event Re-Gifted:

Date:

Got the Same Gift Back: No ... Great!

: Yes ... See Page #   to start over.

The Re-Gifter's Tracking Book

Gift Received:
_____
Event Received:
_____
Received From:
_____
Date:
_____
Re-Gifted To:
_____
Event Re-Gifted:
_____
Date:
_____
Got the Same Gift Back: No ... Great!
_____
                 : Yes ... See Page #   to start over.
_____

Gift Received:
_____
Event Received:
_____
Received From:
_____
Date:
_____
Re-Gifted To:
_____
Event Re-Gifted:
_____
Date:
_____
Got the Same Gift Back: No ... Great!
_____
                 : Yes ... See Page #   to start over.
_____

Gift Received:
_____
Event Received:
_____
Received From:
_____
Date:
_____
Re-Gifted To:
_____
Event Re-Gifted:
_____
Date:
_____
Got the Same Gift Back: No ... Great!
_____
                 : Yes ... See Page #   to start over.
_____

The Re-Gifter's Tracking Book

Gift Received:
_____

Event Received:
_____

Received From:
_____

Date:
_____

Re-Gifted To:
_____

Event Re-Gifted:
_____

Date:
_____

Got the Same Gift Back: No ... Great!
_____
                : Yes ... See Page #_____ to start over.

Gift Received:
_____

Event Received:
_____

Received From:
_____

Date:
_____

Re-Gifted To:
_____

Event Re-Gifted:
_____

Date:
_____

Got the Same Gift Back: No ... Great!
_____
                : Yes ... See Page #_____ to start over.

Gift Received:
_____

Event Received:
_____

Received From:
_____

Date:
_____

Re-Gifted To:
_____

Event Re-Gifted:
_____

Date:
_____

Got the Same Gift Back: No ... Great!
_____
                : Yes ... See Page #_____ to start over.

The Re-Gifter's Tracking Book

Gift Received:
_____
Event Received:
_____
Received From:
_____
Date:
_____
Re-Gifted To:
_____
Event Re-Gifted:
_____
Date:
_____
Got the Same Gift Back: No ... Great!
_____
      : Yes ... See Page #   to start over.
_____

Gift Received:
_____
Event Received:
_____
Received From:
_____
Date:
_____
Re-Gifted To:
_____
Event Re-Gifted:
_____
Date:
_____
Got the Same Gift Back: No ... Great!
_____
      : Yes ... See Page #   to start over.
_____

Gift Received:
_____
Event Received:
_____
Received From:
_____
Date:
_____
Re-Gifted To:
_____
Event Re-Gifted:
_____
Date:
_____
Got the Same Gift Back: No ... Great!
_____
      : Yes ... See Page #   to start over.
_____

The Re-Gifter's Tracking Book

Gift Received:
_____
Event Received:
_____
Received From:
_____
Date:
_____
Re-Gifted To:
_____
Event Re-Gifted:
_____
Date:
_____
Got the Same Gift Back: No ... Great!
_____
           : Yes ... See Page #   to start over.

Gift Received:
_____
Event Received:
_____
Received From:
_____
Date:
_____
Re-Gifted To:
_____
Event Re-Gifted:
_____
Date:
_____
Got the Same Gift Back: No ... Great!
_____
           : Yes ... See Page #   to start over.

Gift Received:
_____
Event Received:
_____
Received From:
_____
Date:
_____
Re-Gifted To:
_____
Event Re-Gifted:
_____
Date:
_____
Got the Same Gift Back: No ... Great!
_____
           : Yes ... See Page #   to start over.

The Re-Gifter's Tracking Book

Gift Received:

Event Received:

Received From:

Date:

Re-Gifted To:

Event Re-Gifted:

Date:

Got the Same Gift Back: No ... Great!

: Yes ... See Page #   to start over.

Gift Received:

Event Received:

Received From:

Date:

Re-Gifted To:

Event Re-Gifted:

Date:

Got the Same Gift Back: No ... Great!

: Yes ... See Page #   to start over.

Gift Received:

Event Received:

Received From:

Date:

Re-Gifted To:

Event Re-Gifted:

Date:

Got the Same Gift Back: No ... Great!

: Yes ... See Page #   to start over.

The Re-Gifter's Tracking Book

Gift Received:
_____

Event Received:
_____

Received From:
_____

Date:
_____

Re-Gifted To:
_____

Event Re-Gifted:
_____

Date:
_____

Got the Same Gift Back: No ... Great!

: Yes ... See Page #_____ to start over.

Gift Received:
_____

Event Received:
_____

Received From:
_____

Date:
_____

Re-Gifted To:
_____

Event Re-Gifted:
_____

Date:
_____

Got the Same Gift Back: No ... Great!

: Yes ... See Page #_____ to start over.

Gift Received:
_____

Event Received:
_____

Received From:
_____

Date:
_____

Re-Gifted To:
_____

Event Re-Gifted:
_____

Date:
_____

Got the Same Gift Back: No ... Great!

: Yes ... See Page #_____ to start over.

The Re-Gifter's Tracking Book

Gift Received:

Event Received:

Received From:

Date:

Re-Gifted To:

Event Re-Gifted:

Date:

Got the Same Gift Back: No ... Great!

: Yes ... See Page #   to start over.

Gift Received:

Event Received:

Received From:

Date:

Re-Gifted To:

Event Re-Gifted:

Date:

Got the Same Gift Back: No ... Great!

: Yes ... See Page #   to start over.

Gift Received:

Event Received:

Received From:

Date:

Re-Gifted To:

Event Re-Gifted:

Date:

Got the Same Gift Back: No ... Great!

: Yes ... See Page #   to start over.

The Re-Gifter's Tracking Book

Gift Received:
_____

Event Received:
_____

Received From:
_____

Date:
_____

Re-Gifted To:
_____

Event Re-Gifted:
_____

Date:
_____

Got the Same Gift Back: No ... Great!
_____

: Yes ... See Page # _____ to start over.
_____

Gift Received:
_____

Event Received:
_____

Received From:
_____

Date:
_____

Re-Gifted To:
_____

Event Re-Gifted:
_____

Date:
_____

Got the Same Gift Back: No ... Great!
_____

: Yes ... See Page # _____ to start over.
_____

Gift Received:
_____

Event Received:
_____

Received From:
_____

Date:
_____

Re-Gifted To:
_____

Event Re-Gifted:
_____

Date:
_____

Got the Same Gift Back: No ... Great!
_____

: Yes ... See Page # _____ to start over.
_____

The Re-Gifter's Tracking Book

Gift Received:
_____
Event Received:
_____
Received From:
_____
Date:
_____
Re-Gifted To:
_____
Event Re-Gifted:
_____
Date:
_____
Got the Same Gift Back: No ... Great!
_____
                : Yes ... See Page #_____ to start over.
_____

Gift Received:
_____
Event Received:
_____
Received From:
_____
Date:
_____
Re-Gifted To:
_____
Event Re-Gifted:
_____
Date:
_____
Got the Same Gift Back: No ... Great!
_____
                : Yes ... See Page #_____ to start over.
_____

Gift Received:
_____
Event Received:
_____
Received From:
_____
Date:
_____
Re-Gifted To:
_____
Event Re-Gifted:
_____
Date:
_____
Got the Same Gift Back: No ... Great!
_____
                : Yes ... See Page #_____ to start over.
_____

The Re-Gifter's Tracking Book

Gift Received:

Event Received:

Received From:

Date:

Re-Gifted To:

Event Re-Gifted:

Date:

Got the Same Gift Back: No ... Great!

: Yes ... See Page #   to start over.

Gift Received:

Event Received:

Received From:

Date:

Re-Gifted To:

Event Re-Gifted:

Date:

Got the Same Gift Back: No ... Great!

: Yes ... See Page #   to start over.

Gift Received:

Event Received:

Received From:

Date:

Re-Gifted To:

Event Re-Gifted:

Date:

Got the Same Gift Back: No ... Great!

: Yes ... See Page #   to start over.

The Re-Gifter's Tracking Book

Gift Received:

Event Received:

Received From:

Date:

Re-Gifted To:

Event Re-Gifted:

Date:

Got the Same Gift Back: No ... Great!

: Yes ... See Page #   to start over.

Gift Received:

Event Received:

Received From:

Date:

Re-Gifted To:

Event Re-Gifted:

Date:

Got the Same Gift Back: No ... Great!

: Yes ... See Page #   to start over.

Gift Received:

Event Received:

Received From:

Date:

Re-Gifted To:

Event Re-Gifted:

Date:

Got the Same Gift Back: No ... Great!

: Yes ... See Page #   to start over.

The Re-Gifter's Tracking Book

Gift Received:

Event Received:

Received From:

Date:

Re-Gifted To:

Event Re-Gifted:

Date:

Got the Same Gift Back: No ... Great!

                    : Yes ... See Page #   to start over.

Gift Received:

Event Received:

Received From:

Date:

Re-Gifted To:

Event Re-Gifted:

Date:

Got the Same Gift Back: No ... Great!

                    : Yes ... See Page #   to start over.

Gift Received:

Event Received:

Received From:

Date:

Re-Gifted To:

Event Re-Gifted:

Date:

Got the Same Gift Back: No ... Great!

                    : Yes ... See Page #   to start over.

The Re-Gifter's Tracking Book

Gift Received:
_____

Event Received:
_____

Received From:
_____

Date:
_____

Re-Gifted To:
_____

Event Re-Gifted:
_____

Date:
_____

Got the Same Gift Back: No ... Great!
_____

        : Yes ... See Page # _____ to start over.

Gift Received:
_____

Event Received:
_____

Received From:
_____

Date:
_____

Re-Gifted To:
_____

Event Re-Gifted:
_____

Date:
_____

Got the Same Gift Back: No ... Great!
_____

        : Yes ... See Page # _____ to start over.

Gift Received:
_____

Event Received:
_____

Received From:
_____

Date:
_____

Re-Gifted To:
_____

Event Re-Gifted:
_____

Date:
_____

Got the Same Gift Back: No ... Great!
_____

        : Yes ... See Page # _____ to start over.

The Re-Gifter's Tracking Book

Gift Received:

Event Received:

Received From:

Date:

Re-Gifted To:

Event Re-Gifted:

Date:

Got the Same Gift Back: No ... Great!

                     : Yes ... See Page #   to start over.

Gift Received:

Event Received:

Received From:

Date:

Re-Gifted To:

Event Re-Gifted:

Date:

Got the Same Gift Back: No ... Great!

                     : Yes ... See Page #   to start over.

Gift Received:

Event Received:

Received From:

Date:

Re-Gifted To:

Event Re-Gifted:

Date:

Got the Same Gift Back: No ... Great!

                     : Yes ... See Page #   to start over.

The Re-Gifter's Tracking Book

Gift Received:
_____

Event Received:
_____

Received From:
_____

Date:
_____

Re-Gifted To:
_____

Event Re-Gifted:
_____

Date:
_____

Got the Same Gift Back: No ... Great!
_____
: Yes ... See Page # _____ to start over.

Gift Received:
_____

Event Received:
_____

Received From:
_____

Date:
_____

Re-Gifted To:
_____

Event Re-Gifted:
_____

Date:
_____

Got the Same Gift Back: No ... Great!
_____
: Yes ... See Page # _____ to start over.

Gift Received:
_____

Event Received:
_____

Received From:
_____

Date:
_____

Re-Gifted To:
_____

Event Re-Gifted:
_____

Date:
_____

Got the Same Gift Back: No ... Great!
_____
: Yes ... See Page # _____ to start over.

The Re-Gifter's Tracking Book

Gift Received:
_____

Event Received:
_____

Received From:
_____

Date:
_____

Re-Gifted To:
_____

Event Re-Gifted:
_____

Date:
_____

Got the Same Gift Back: No ... Great!

           : Yes ... See Page #_____ to start over.

Gift Received:
_____

Event Received:
_____

Received From:
_____

Date:
_____

Re-Gifted To:
_____

Event Re-Gifted:
_____

Date:
_____

Got the Same Gift Back: No ... Great!

           : Yes ... See Page #_____ to start over.

Gift Received:
_____

Event Received:
_____

Received From:
_____

Date:
_____

Re-Gifted To:
_____

Event Re-Gifted:
_____

Date:
_____

Got the Same Gift Back: No ... Great!

           : Yes ... See Page #_____ to start over.

The Re-Gifter's Tracking Book

Gift Received:
_____

Event Received:
_____

Received From:
_____

Date:
_____

Re-Gifted To:
_____

Event Re-Gifted:
_____

Date:
_____

Got the Same Gift Back: No ... Great!
_____

                  : Yes ... See Page #   to start over.
_____

Gift Received:
_____

Event Received:
_____

Received From:
_____

Date:
_____

Re-Gifted To:
_____

Event Re-Gifted:
_____

Date:
_____

Got the Same Gift Back: No ... Great!
_____

                  : Yes ... See Page #   to start over.
_____

Gift Received:
_____

Event Received:
_____

Received From:
_____

Date:
_____

Re-Gifted To:
_____

Event Re-Gifted:
_____

Date:
_____

Got the Same Gift Back: No ... Great!
_____

                  : Yes ... See Page #   to start over.
_____

The Re-Gifter's Tracking Book

Gift Received:
_____
Event Received:
_____
Received From:
_____
Date:
_____
Re-Gifted To:
_____
Event Re-Gifted:
_____
Date:
_____
Got the Same Gift Back: No ... Great!
_____
                     : Yes ... See Page #   to start over.

Gift Received:
_____
Event Received:
_____
Received From:
_____
Date:
_____
Re-Gifted To:
_____
Event Re-Gifted:
_____
Date:
_____
Got the Same Gift Back: No ... Great!
_____
                     : Yes ... See Page #   to start over.

Gift Received:
_____
Event Received:
_____
Received From:
_____
Date:
_____
Re-Gifted To:
_____
Event Re-Gifted:
_____
Date:
_____
Got the Same Gift Back: No ... Great!
_____
                     : Yes ... See Page #   to start over.

The Re-Gifter's Tracking Book

Gift Received:
_____

Event Received:
_____

Received From:
_____

Date:
_____

Re-Gifted To:
_____

Event Re-Gifted:
_____

Date:
_____

Got the Same Gift Back: No ... Great!
_____
                    : Yes ... See Page #   to start over.

Gift Received:
_____

Event Received:
_____

Received From:
_____

Date:
_____

Re-Gifted To:
_____

Event Re-Gifted:
_____

Date:
_____

Got the Same Gift Back: No ... Great!
_____
                    : Yes ... See Page #   to start over.

Gift Received:
_____

Event Received:
_____

Received From:
_____

Date:
_____

Re-Gifted To:
_____

Event Re-Gifted:
_____

Date:
_____

Got the Same Gift Back: No ... Great!
_____
                    : Yes ... See Page #   to start over.

The Re-Gifter's Tracking Book

Gift Received: _____

Event Received: _____

Received From: _____

Date: _____

Re-Gifted To: _____

Event Re-Gifted: _____

Date: _____

Got the Same Gift Back: No ... Great!

                 : Yes ... See Page # _____ to start over.

Gift Received: _____

Event Received: _____

Received From: _____

Date: _____

Re-Gifted To: _____

Event Re-Gifted: _____

Date: _____

Got the Same Gift Back: No ... Great!

                 : Yes ... See Page # _____ to start over.

Gift Received: _____

Event Received: _____

Received From: _____

Date: _____

Re-Gifted To: _____

Event Re-Gifted: _____

Date: _____

Got the Same Gift Back: No ... Great!

                 : Yes ... See Page # _____ to start over.

The Re-Gifter's Tracking Book

Gift Received:
_____

Event Received:
_____

Received From:
_____

Date:
_____

Re-Gifted To:
_____

Event Re-Gifted:
_____

Date:
_____

Got the Same Gift Back: No ... Great!

: Yes ... See Page # _____ to start over.

Gift Received:
_____

Event Received:
_____

Received From:
_____

Date:
_____

Re-Gifted To:
_____

Event Re-Gifted:
_____

Date:
_____

Got the Same Gift Back: No ... Great!

: Yes ... See Page # _____ to start over.

Gift Received:
_____

Event Received:
_____

Received From:
_____

Date:
_____

Re-Gifted To:
_____

Event Re-Gifted:
_____

Date:
_____

Got the Same Gift Back: No ... Great!

: Yes ... See Page # _____ to start over.

The Re-Gifter's Tracking Book

Gift Received:
_____

Event Received:
_____

Received From:
_____

Date:
_____

Re-Gifted To:
_____

Event Re-Gifted:
_____

Date:
_____

Got the Same Gift Back: No ... Great!
_____

                   : Yes ... See Page #_____ to start over.
_____

Gift Received:
_____

Event Received:
_____

Received From:
_____

Date:
_____

Re-Gifted To:
_____

Event Re-Gifted:
_____

Date:
_____

Got the Same Gift Back: No ... Great!
_____

                   : Yes ... See Page #_____ to start over.
_____

Gift Received:
_____

Event Received:
_____

Received From:
_____

Date:
_____

Re-Gifted To:
_____

Event Re-Gifted:
_____

Date:
_____

Got the Same Gift Back: No ... Great!
_____

                   : Yes ... See Page #_____ to start over.
_____

The Re-Gifter's Tracking Book

Gift Received:

Event Received:

Received From:

Date:

Re-Gifted To:

Event Re-Gifted:

Date:

Got the Same Gift Back: No ... Great!

                    : Yes ... See Page #   to start over.

Gift Received:

Event Received:

Received From:

Date:

Re-Gifted To:

Event Re-Gifted:

Date:

Got the Same Gift Back: No ... Great!

                    : Yes ... See Page #   to start over.

Gift Received:

Event Received:

Received From:

Date:

Re-Gifted To:

Event Re-Gifted:

Date:

Got the Same Gift Back: No ... Great!

                    : Yes ... See Page #   to start over.

The Re-Gifter's Tracking Book

Gift Received:
_____

Event Received:
_____

Received From:
_____

Date:
_____

Re-Gifted To:
_____

Event Re-Gifted:
_____

Date:
_____

Got the Same Gift Back: No ... Great!
_____

              : Yes ... See Page #   to start over.

Gift Received:
_____

Event Received:
_____

Received From:
_____

Date:
_____

Re-Gifted To:
_____

Event Re-Gifted:
_____

Date:
_____

Got the Same Gift Back: No ... Great!
_____

              : Yes ... See Page #   to start over.

Gift Received:
_____

Event Received:
_____

Received From:
_____

Date:
_____

Re-Gifted To:
_____

Event Re-Gifted:
_____

Date:
_____

Got the Same Gift Back: No ... Great!
_____

              : Yes ... See Page #   to start over.

The Re-Gifter's Tracking Book

Gift Received: _____

Event Received: _____

Received From: _____

Date: _____

Re-Gifted To: _____

Event Re-Gifted: _____

Date: _____

Got the Same Gift Back: No ... Great!

                  : Yes ... See Page #_____ to start over.

Gift Received: _____

Event Received: _____

Received From: _____

Date: _____

Re-Gifted To: _____

Event Re-Gifted: _____

Date: _____

Got the Same Gift Back: No ... Great!

                  : Yes ... See Page #_____ to start over.

Gift Received: _____

Event Received: _____

Received From: _____

Date: _____

Re-Gifted To: _____

Event Re-Gifted: _____

Date: _____

Got the Same Gift Back: No ... Great!

                  : Yes ... See Page #_____ to start over.

The Re-Gifter's Tracking Book

Gift Received:
_____

Event Received:
_____

Received From:
_____

Date:
_____

Re-Gifted To:
_____

Event Re-Gifted:
_____

Date:
_____

Got the Same Gift Back: No ... Great!

: Yes ... See Page #_____ to start over.

Gift Received:
_____

Event Received:
_____

Received From:
_____

Date:
_____

Re-Gifted To:
_____

Event Re-Gifted:
_____

Date:
_____

Got the Same Gift Back: No ... Great!

: Yes ... See Page #_____ to start over.

Gift Received:
_____

Event Received:
_____

Received From:
_____

Date:
_____

Re-Gifted To:
_____

Event Re-Gifted:
_____

Date:
_____

Got the Same Gift Back: No ... Great!

: Yes ... See Page #_____ to start over.

The Re-Gifter's Tracking Book

Gift Received:

Event Received:

Received From:

Date:

Re-Gifted To:

Event Re-Gifted:

Date:

Got the Same Gift Back: No ... Great!

                : Yes ... See Page #   to start over.

Gift Received:

Event Received:

Received From:

Date:

Re-Gifted To:

Event Re-Gifted:

Date:

Got the Same Gift Back: No ... Great!

                : Yes ... See Page #   to start over.

Gift Received:

Event Received:

Received From:

Date:

Re-Gifted To:

Event Re-Gifted:

Date:

Got the Same Gift Back: No ... Great!

                : Yes ... See Page #   to start over.

The Re-Gifter's Tracking Book

Gift Received:
_____
Event Received:
_____
Received From:
_____
Date:
_____
Re-Gifted To:
_____
Event Re-Gifted:
_____
Date:
_____
Got the Same Gift Back: No ... Great!
_____
: Yes ... See Page #_____ to start over.
_____

Gift Received:
_____
Event Received:
_____
Received From:
_____
Date:
_____
Re-Gifted To:
_____
Event Re-Gifted:
_____
Date:
_____
Got the Same Gift Back: No ... Great!
_____
: Yes ... See Page #_____ to start over.
_____

Gift Received:
_____
Event Received:
_____
Received From:
_____
Date:
_____
Re-Gifted To:
_____
Event Re-Gifted:
_____
Date:
_____
Got the Same Gift Back: No ... Great!
_____
: Yes ... See Page #_____ to start over.
_____

The Re-Gifter's Tracking Book

Gift Received:
_____
Event Received:
_____
Received From:
_____
Date:
_____
Re-Gifted To:
_____
Event Re-Gifted:
_____
Date:
_____
Got the Same Gift Back: No ... Great!
_____
           : Yes ... See Page #   to start over.

Gift Received:
_____
Event Received:
_____
Received From:
_____
Date:
_____
Re-Gifted To:
_____
Event Re-Gifted:
_____
Date:
_____
Got the Same Gift Back: No ... Great!
_____
           : Yes ... See Page #   to start over.

Gift Received:
_____
Event Received:
_____
Received From:
_____
Date:
_____
Re-Gifted To:
_____
Event Re-Gifted:
_____
Date:
_____
Got the Same Gift Back: No ... Great!
_____
           : Yes ... See Page #   to start over.

The Re-Gifter's Tracking Book

Gift Received:
_____

Event Received:
_____

Received From:
_____

Date:
_____

Re-Gifted To:
_____

Event Re-Gifted:
_____

Date:
_____

Got the Same Gift Back: No ... Great!

: Yes ... See Page #   to start over.

Gift Received:
_____

Event Received:
_____

Received From:
_____

Date:
_____

Re-Gifted To:
_____

Event Re-Gifted:
_____

Date:
_____

Got the Same Gift Back: No ... Great!

: Yes ... See Page #   to start over.

Gift Received:
_____

Event Received:
_____

Received From:
_____

Date:
_____

Re-Gifted To:
_____

Event Re-Gifted:
_____

Date:
_____

Got the Same Gift Back: No ... Great!

: Yes ... See Page #   to start over.

The Re-Gifter's Tracking Book

Gift Received:

Event Received:

Received From:

Date:

Re-Gifted To:

Event Re-Gifted:

Date:

Got the Same Gift Back: No ... Great!

: Yes ... See Page #   to start over.

Gift Received:

Event Received:

Received From:

Date:

Re-Gifted To:

Event Re-Gifted:

Date:

Got the Same Gift Back: No ... Great!

: Yes ... See Page #   to start over.

Gift Received:

Event Received:

Received From:

Date:

Re-Gifted To:

Event Re-Gifted:

Date:

Got the Same Gift Back: No ... Great!

: Yes ... See Page #   to start over.

The Re-Gifter's Tracking Book

Gift Received:
_____

Event Received:
_____

Received From:
_____

Date:
_____

Re-Gifted To:
_____

Event Re-Gifted:
_____

Date:
_____

Got the Same Gift Back: No ... Great!

       : Yes ... See Page #_____ to start over.

Gift Received:
_____

Event Received:
_____

Received From:
_____

Date:
_____

Re-Gifted To:
_____

Event Re-Gifted:
_____

Date:
_____

Got the Same Gift Back: No ... Great!

       : Yes ... See Page #_____ to start over.

Gift Received:
_____

Event Received:
_____

Received From:
_____

Date:
_____

Re-Gifted To:
_____

Event Re-Gifted:
_____

Date:
_____

Got the Same Gift Back: No ... Great!

       : Yes ... See Page #_____ to start over.

The Re-Gifter's Tracking Book

Gift Received:

Event Received:

Received From:

Date:

Re-Gifted To:

Event Re-Gifted:

Date:

Got the Same Gift Back: No ... Great!

: Yes ... See Page #   to start over.

Gift Received:

Event Received:

Received From:

Date:

Re-Gifted To:

Event Re-Gifted:

Date:

Got the Same Gift Back: No ... Great!

: Yes ... See Page #   to start over.

Gift Received:

Event Received:

Received From:

Date:

Re-Gifted To:

Event Re-Gifted:

Date:

Got the Same Gift Back: No ... Great!

: Yes ... See Page #   to start over.

The Re-Gifter's Tracking Book

Gift Received:
_____
Event Received:
_____
Received From:
_____
Date:
_____
Re-Gifted To:
_____
Event Re-Gifted:
_____
Date:
_____
Got the Same Gift Back: No ... Great!
_____
                  : Yes ... See Page #_____ to start over.

Gift Received:
_____
Event Received:
_____
Received From:
_____
Date:
_____
Re-Gifted To:
_____
Event Re-Gifted:
_____
Date:
_____
Got the Same Gift Back: No ... Great!
_____
                  : Yes ... See Page #_____ to start over.

Gift Received:
_____
Event Received:
_____
Received From:
_____
Date:
_____
Re-Gifted To:
_____
Event Re-Gifted:
_____
Date:
_____
Got the Same Gift Back: No ... Great!
_____
                  : Yes ... See Page #_____ to start over.

The Re-Gifter's Tracking Book

Gift Received:
_____
Event Received:
_____
Received From:
_____
Date:
_____
Re-Gifted To:
_____
Event Re-Gifted:
_____
Date:
_____
Got the Same Gift Back: No ... Great!
_____
                     : Yes ... See Page #   to start over.
_____

Gift Received:
_____
Event Received:
_____
Received From:
_____
Date:
_____
Re-Gifted To:
_____
Event Re-Gifted:
_____
Date:
_____
Got the Same Gift Back: No ... Great!
_____
                     : Yes ... See Page #   to start over.
_____

Gift Received:
_____
Event Received:
_____
Received From:
_____
Date:
_____
Re-Gifted To:
_____
Event Re-Gifted:
_____
Date:
_____
Got the Same Gift Back: No ... Great!
_____
                     : Yes ... See Page #   to start over.
_____

The Re-Gifter's Tracking Book

Gift Received:
_____

Event Received:
_____

Received From:
_____

Date:
_____

Re-Gifted To:
_____

Event Re-Gifted:
_____

Date:
_____

Got the Same Gift Back: No ... Great!

: Yes ... See Page #_____ to start over.

Gift Received:
_____

Event Received:
_____

Received From:
_____

Date:
_____

Re-Gifted To:
_____

Event Re-Gifted:
_____

Date:
_____

Got the Same Gift Back: No ... Great!

: Yes ... See Page #_____ to start over.

Gift Received:
_____

Event Received:
_____

Received From:
_____

Date:
_____

Re-Gifted To:
_____

Event Re-Gifted:
_____

Date:
_____

Got the Same Gift Back: No ... Great!

: Yes ... See Page #_____ to start over.

The Re-Gifter's Tracking Book

Gift Received:

Event Received:

Received From:

Date:

Re-Gifted To:

Event Re-Gifted:

Date:

Got the Same Gift Back: No ... Great!

                    : Yes ... See Page #   to start over.

Gift Received:

Event Received:

Received From:

Date:

Re-Gifted To:

Event Re-Gifted:

Date:

Got the Same Gift Back: No ... Great!

                    : Yes ... See Page #   to start over.

Gift Received:

Event Received:

Received From:

Date:

Re-Gifted To:

Event Re-Gifted:

Date:

Got the Same Gift Back: No ... Great!

                    : Yes ... See Page #   to start over.

The Re-Gifter's Tracking Book

Gift Received:
_____

Event Received:
_____

Received From:
_____

Date:
_____

Re-Gifted To:
_____

Event Re-Gifted:
_____

Date:
_____

Got the Same Gift Back: No ... Great!
_____
                    : Yes ... See Page #   to start over.

Gift Received:
_____

Event Received:
_____

Received From:
_____

Date:
_____

Re-Gifted To:
_____

Event Re-Gifted:
_____

Date:
_____

Got the Same Gift Back: No ... Great!
_____
                    : Yes ... See Page #   to start over.

Gift Received:
_____

Event Received:
_____

Received From:
_____

Date:
_____

Re-Gifted To:
_____

Event Re-Gifted:
_____

Date:
_____

Got the Same Gift Back: No ... Great!
_____
                    : Yes ... See Page #   to start over.

The Re-Gifter's Tracking Book

Gift Received:

Event Received:

Received From:

Date:

Re-Gifted To:

Event Re-Gifted:

Date:

Got the Same Gift Back: No ... Great!

                   : Yes ... See Page #   to start over.

Gift Received:

Event Received:

Received From:

Date:

Re-Gifted To:

Event Re-Gifted:

Date:

Got the Same Gift Back: No ... Great!

                   : Yes ... See Page #   to start over.

Gift Received:

Event Received:

Received From:

Date:

Re-Gifted To:

Event Re-Gifted:

Date:

Got the Same Gift Back: No ... Great!

                   : Yes ... See Page #   to start over.

The Re-Gifter's Tracking Book

Gift Received: _____

Event Received: _____

Received From: _____

Date: _____

Re-Gifted To: _____

Event Re-Gifted: _____

Date: _____

Got the Same Gift Back: No ... Great! _____

                    : Yes ... See Page # _____ to start over.

Gift Received: _____

Event Received: _____

Received From: _____

Date: _____

Re-Gifted To: _____

Event Re-Gifted: _____

Date: _____

Got the Same Gift Back: No ... Great! _____

                    : Yes ... See Page # _____ to start over.

Gift Received: _____

Event Received: _____

Received From: _____

Date: _____

Re-Gifted To: _____

Event Re-Gifted: _____

Date: _____

Got the Same Gift Back: No ... Great! _____

                    : Yes ... See Page # _____ to start over.

The Re-Gifter's Tracking Book

Gift Received:
_____

Event Received:
_____

Received From:
_____

Date:
_____

Re-Gifted To:
_____

Event Re-Gifted:
_____

Date:
_____

Got the Same Gift Back: No ... Great!

: Yes ... See Page #   to start over.
_____

Gift Received:
_____

Event Received:
_____

Received From:
_____

Date:
_____

Re-Gifted To:
_____

Event Re-Gifted:
_____

Date:
_____

Got the Same Gift Back: No ... Great!

: Yes ... See Page #   to start over.
_____

Gift Received:
_____

Event Received:
_____

Received From:
_____

Date:
_____

Re-Gifted To:
_____

Event Re-Gifted:
_____

Date:
_____

Got the Same Gift Back: No ... Great!

: Yes ... See Page #   to start over.
_____

The Re-Gifter's Tracking Book

Gift Received:
_____

Event Received:
_____

Received From:
_____

Date:
_____

Re-Gifted To:
_____

Event Re-Gifted:
_____

Date:
_____

Got the Same Gift Back: No ... Great!

               : Yes ... See Page #   to start over.

Gift Received:
_____

Event Received:
_____

Received From:
_____

Date:
_____

Re-Gifted To:
_____

Event Re-Gifted:
_____

Date:
_____

Got the Same Gift Back: No ... Great!

               : Yes ... See Page #   to start over.

Gift Received:
_____

Event Received:
_____

Received From:
_____

Date:
_____

Re-Gifted To:
_____

Event Re-Gifted:
_____

Date:
_____

Got the Same Gift Back: No ... Great!

               : Yes ... See Page #   to start over.

The Re-Gifter's Tracking Book

Gift Received: _____

Event Received: _____

Received From: _____

Date: _____

Re-Gifted To: _____

Event Re-Gifted: _____

Date: _____

Got the Same Gift Back: No ... Great!

                     : Yes ... See Page #   to start over.

Gift Received: _____

Event Received: _____

Received From: _____

Date: _____

Re-Gifted To: _____

Event Re-Gifted: _____

Date: _____

Got the Same Gift Back: No ... Great!

                     : Yes ... See Page #   to start over.

Gift Received: _____

Event Received: _____

Received From: _____

Date: _____

Re-Gifted To: _____

Event Re-Gifted: _____

Date: _____

Got the Same Gift Back: No ... Great!

                     : Yes ... See Page #   to start over.

The Re-Gifter's Tracking Book

Gift Received:
_____
Event Received:
_____
Received From:
_____
Date:
_____
Re-Gifted To:
_____
Event Re-Gifted:
_____
Date:
_____
Got the Same Gift Back: No ... Great!
_____
                    : Yes ... See Page #_____ to start over.
_____

Gift Received:
_____
Event Received:
_____
Received From:
_____
Date:
_____
Re-Gifted To:
_____
Event Re-Gifted:
_____
Date:
_____
Got the Same Gift Back: No ... Great!
_____
                    : Yes ... See Page #_____ to start over.
_____

Gift Received:
_____
Event Received:
_____
Received From:
_____
Date:
_____
Re-Gifted To:
_____
Event Re-Gifted:
_____
Date:
_____
Got the Same Gift Back: No ... Great!
_____
                    : Yes ... See Page #_____ to start over.
_____

The Re-Gifter's Tracking Book

Gift Received:

Event Received:

Received From:

Date:

Re-Gifted To:

Event Re-Gifted:

Date:

Got the Same Gift Back: No ... Great!

                 : Yes ... See Page #   to start over.

Gift Received:

Event Received:

Received From:

Date:

Re-Gifted To:

Event Re-Gifted:

Date:

Got the Same Gift Back: No ... Great!

                 : Yes ... See Page #   to start over.

Gift Received:

Event Received:

Received From:

Date:

Re-Gifted To:

Event Re-Gifted:

Date:

Got the Same Gift Back: No ... Great!

                 : Yes ... See Page #   to start over.

The Re-Gifter's Tracking Book

Gift Received:
_____
Event Received:
_____
Received From:
_____
Date:
_____
Re-Gifted To:
_____
Event Re-Gifted:
_____
Date:
_____
Got the Same Gift Back: No ... Great!
_____
                    : Yes ... See Page #   to start over.
_____

Gift Received:
_____
Event Received:
_____
Received From:
_____
Date:
_____
Re-Gifted To:
_____
Event Re-Gifted:
_____
Date:
_____
Got the Same Gift Back: No ... Great!
_____
                    : Yes ... See Page #   to start over.
_____

Gift Received:
_____
Event Received:
_____
Received From:
_____
Date:
_____
Re-Gifted To:
_____
Event Re-Gifted:
_____
Date:
_____
Got the Same Gift Back: No ... Great!
_____
                    : Yes ... See Page #   to start over.
_____

The Re-Gifter's Tracking Book

Gift Received:
_____

Event Received:
_____

Received From:
_____

Date:
_____

Re-Gifted To:
_____

Event Re-Gifted:
_____

Date:
_____

Got the Same Gift Back: No ... Great!

              : Yes ... See Page #   to start over.

Gift Received:
_____

Event Received:
_____

Received From:
_____

Date:
_____

Re-Gifted To:
_____

Event Re-Gifted:
_____

Date:
_____

Got the Same Gift Back: No ... Great!

              : Yes ... See Page #   to start over.

Gift Received:
_____

Event Received:
_____

Received From:
_____

Date:
_____

Re-Gifted To:
_____

Event Re-Gifted:
_____

Date:
_____

Got the Same Gift Back: No ... Great!

              : Yes ... See Page #   to start over.

The Re-Gifter's Tracking Book

Gift Received:
_____
Event Received:
_____
Received From:
_____
Date:
_____
Re-Gifted To:
_____
Event Re-Gifted:
_____
Date:
_____
Got the Same Gift Back: No ... Great!
                   : Yes ... See Page #   to start over.

Gift Received:
_____
Event Received:
_____
Received From:
_____
Date:
_____
Re-Gifted To:
_____
Event Re-Gifted:
_____
Date:
_____
Got the Same Gift Back: No ... Great!
                   : Yes ... See Page #   to start over.

Gift Received:
_____
Event Received:
_____
Received From:
_____
Date:
_____
Re-Gifted To:
_____
Event Re-Gifted:
_____
Date:
_____
Got the Same Gift Back: No ... Great!
                   : Yes ... See Page #   to start over.

The Re-Gifter's Tracking Book

Gift Received:
_____
Event Received:
_____
Received From:
_____
Date:
_____
Re-Gifted To:
_____
Event Re-Gifted:
_____
Date:
_____
Got the Same Gift Back: No ... Great!
_____
                    : Yes ... See Page #_____ to start over.

Gift Received:
_____
Event Received:
_____
Received From:
_____
Date:
_____
Re-Gifted To:
_____
Event Re-Gifted:
_____
Date:
_____
Got the Same Gift Back: No ... Great!
_____
                    : Yes ... See Page #_____ to start over.

Gift Received:
_____
Event Received:
_____
Received From:
_____
Date:
_____
Re-Gifted To:
_____
Event Re-Gifted:
_____
Date:
_____
Got the Same Gift Back: No ... Great!
_____
                    : Yes ... See Page #_____ to start over.

The Re-Gifter's Tracking Book

Gift Received:
_____
Event Received:
_____
Received From:
_____
Date:
_____
Re-Gifted To:
_____
Event Re-Gifted:
_____
Date:
_____
Got the Same Gift Back: No ... Great!
_____
             : Yes ... See Page #_____ to start over.

Gift Received:
_____
Event Received:
_____
Received From:
_____
Date:
_____
Re-Gifted To:
_____
Event Re-Gifted:
_____
Date:
_____
Got the Same Gift Back: No ... Great!
_____
             : Yes ... See Page #_____ to start over.

Gift Received:
_____
Event Received:
_____
Received From:
_____
Date:
_____
Re-Gifted To:
_____
Event Re-Gifted:
_____
Date:
_____
Got the Same Gift Back: No ... Great!
_____
             : Yes ... See Page #_____ to start over.

The Re-Gifter's Tracking Book

Gift Received:
_____

Event Received:
_____

Received From:
_____

Date:
_____

Re-Gifted To:
_____

Event Re-Gifted:
_____

Date:
_____

Got the Same Gift Back: No ... Great!

: Yes ... See Page #_____ to start over.

Gift Received:
_____

Event Received:
_____

Received From:
_____

Date:
_____

Re-Gifted To:
_____

Event Re-Gifted:
_____

Date:
_____

Got the Same Gift Back: No ... Great!

: Yes ... See Page #_____ to start over.

Gift Received:
_____

Event Received:
_____

Received From:
_____

Date:
_____

Re-Gifted To:
_____

Event Re-Gifted:
_____

Date:
_____

Got the Same Gift Back: No ... Great!

: Yes ... See Page #_____ to start over.

The Re-Gifter's Tracking Book

Gift Received:
_____
Event Received:
_____
Received From:
_____
Date:
_____
Re-Gifted To:
_____
Event Re-Gifted:
_____
Date:
_____
Got the Same Gift Back: No ... Great!
_____
                : Yes ... See Page #   to start over.

Gift Received:
_____
Event Received:
_____
Received From:
_____
Date:
_____
Re-Gifted To:
_____
Event Re-Gifted:
_____
Date:
_____
Got the Same Gift Back: No ... Great!
_____
                : Yes ... See Page #   to start over.

Gift Received:
_____
Event Received:
_____
Received From:
_____
Date:
_____
Re-Gifted To:
_____
Event Re-Gifted:
_____
Date:
_____
Got the Same Gift Back: No ... Great!
_____
                : Yes ... See Page #   to start over.

The Re-Gifter's Tracking Book

Gift Received:
_____

Event Received:
_____

Received From:
_____

Date:
_____

Re-Gifted To:
_____

Event Re-Gifted:
_____

Date:
_____

Got the Same Gift Back: No ... Great!
_____

                : Yes ... See Page #   to start over.

Gift Received:
_____

Event Received:
_____

Received From:
_____

Date:
_____

Re-Gifted To:
_____

Event Re-Gifted:
_____

Date:
_____

Got the Same Gift Back: No ... Great!
_____

                : Yes ... See Page #   to start over.

Gift Received:
_____

Event Received:
_____

Received From:
_____

Date:
_____

Re-Gifted To:
_____

Event Re-Gifted:
_____

Date:
_____

Got the Same Gift Back: No ... Great!
_____

                : Yes ... See Page #   to start over.

The Re-Gifter's Tracking Book

Gift Received: _____
_____
Event Received: _____
Received From: _____
Date: _____
Re-Gifted To: _____
Event Re-Gifted: _____
Date: _____
Got the Same Gift Back: No ... Great!
: Yes ... See Page #_____ to start over.

Gift Received: _____
_____
Event Received: _____
Received From: _____
Date: _____
Re-Gifted To: _____
Event Re-Gifted: _____
Date: _____
Got the Same Gift Back: No ... Great!
: Yes ... See Page #_____ to start over.

Gift Received: _____
_____
Event Received: _____
Received From: _____
Date: _____
Re-Gifted To: _____
Event Re-Gifted: _____
Date: _____
Got the Same Gift Back: No ... Great!
: Yes ... See Page #_____ to start over.

The Re-Gifter's Tracking Book

Gift Received:
_____

Event Received:
_____

Received From:
_____

Date:
_____

Re-Gifted To:
_____

Event Re-Gifted:
_____

Date:
_____

Got the Same Gift Back: No ... Great!
_____

                 : Yes ... See Page #   to start over.
_____

Gift Received:
_____

Event Received:
_____

Received From:
_____

Date:
_____

Re-Gifted To:
_____

Event Re-Gifted:
_____

Date:
_____

Got the Same Gift Back: No ... Great!
_____

                 : Yes ... See Page #   to start over.
_____

Gift Received:
_____

Event Received:
_____

Received From:
_____

Date:
_____

Re-Gifted To:
_____

Event Re-Gifted:
_____

Date:
_____

Got the Same Gift Back: No ... Great!
_____

                 : Yes ... See Page #   to start over.
_____

The Re-Gifter's Tracking Book

Gift Received:
_____
Event Received:
_____
Received From:
_____
Date:
_____
Re-Gifted To:
_____
Event Re-Gifted:
_____
Date:
_____
Got the Same Gift Back: No ... Great!
_____ : Yes ... See Page #_____ to start over.

Gift Received:
_____
Event Received:
_____
Received From:
_____
Date:
_____
Re-Gifted To:
_____
Event Re-Gifted:
_____
Date:
_____
Got the Same Gift Back: No ... Great!
_____ : Yes ... See Page #_____ to start over.

Gift Received:
_____
Event Received:
_____
Received From:
_____
Date:
_____
Re-Gifted To:
_____
Event Re-Gifted:
_____
Date:
_____
Got the Same Gift Back: No ... Great!
_____ : Yes ... See Page #_____ to start over.

The Re-Gifter's Tracking Book

Gift Received:
_____

Event Received:
_____

Received From:
_____

Date:
_____

Re-Gifted To:
_____

Event Re-Gifted:
_____

Date:
_____

Got the Same Gift Back: No ... Great!

: Yes ... See Page #_____ to start over.

Gift Received:
_____

Event Received:
_____

Received From:
_____

Date:
_____

Re-Gifted To:
_____

Event Re-Gifted:
_____

Date:
_____

Got the Same Gift Back: No ... Great!

: Yes ... See Page #_____ to start over.

Gift Received:
_____

Event Received:
_____

Received From:
_____

Date:
_____

Re-Gifted To:
_____

Event Re-Gifted:
_____

Date:
_____

Got the Same Gift Back: No ... Great!

: Yes ... See Page #_____ to start over.